Dedicated to all the men and women who have given their lives
protecting our right to life, liberty, and the pursuit of happiness.

Thank you to my brother Stephen, who has been
a lifelong source of inspiration and encouragement.

Book design by Sara Gillingham.
Typeset in Artcraft.
The illustrations in this book were rendered in ink and watercolor.
Manufactured in China.

Library of Congress Cataloging-in-Publication Data
Robertson, Chris, 1958-
Little Miss Liberty / by Chris Robertson.
p. cm.
Summary: When Little Miss Liberty, a very special child, outgrows her Paris home,
she sets out on a journey in search of a place she can call her own.
ISBN 0-8118-4669-5
1. Statue of Liberty (New York, N.Y.)–Juvenile fiction. [1. Statue of Liberty (New York, N.Y.)–Fiction.] I. Title.
PZ7.R54468Li 2005
[E]–dc22
2004013363

Distributed in Canada by Raincoast Books
9050 Shaughnessy Street, Vancouver, British Columbia V6P 6E5

10 9 8 7 6 5 4 3 2 1

Chronicle Books LLC
85 Second Street, San Francisco, California 94105

www.chroniclekids.com

Little Miss Liberty

by Chris Robertson

chronicle books · san francisco

On an early July morning, in the city of Paris,

the cry of a newborn
baby girl was heard.

The name given to her
was Little Miss Liberty.

The minute she was placed in her mother's arms,
it was obvious she was special.

To begin with, her coloring
was a little on the green side.

Secondly, unlike most babies, Little Miss Liberty
could stand as soon as she was born.

In addition, with every day that passed,
she grew several inches.

Her parents had a hard time finding clothes that would fit her.

Finally, they gave up and wrapped her in a queen-size bedsheet.

Little Miss Liberty had an insatiable appetite. Not just for food, but also for knowledge. She read anything and everything . . .

from books to cereal boxes,
from billboards to maps,

from comic books to her father's newspaper.

She read and grew,

grew and read,

and read and grew
some more.

One day, her mother
took her shopping.

Little Miss Liberty picked out
the most peculiar-looking hat.

She loved it so,
she wore it every day.

When she started school, the other children
didn't quite know what to think of her.

But she was of strong will and character,
and when the teacher asked the class a question,

Little Miss Liberty's arm would shoot skyward, like a rocket.
It seemed to be frozen straight up in the air.

Little Miss Liberty was a friend to all. She was especially kind to those who felt different or misunderstood, lonely or sad.

Eventually Little Miss Liberty finished school.
By then, she found she had outgrown almost everything,

 her bed,

her table and chair,

her house,

even the city she had always known and loved.

Always a child of independence, Little Miss Liberty knew
there was a place in the world she was meant to be.

So one night, she packed up her books, lit a torch,
and, with her parents' blessing, set off on a journey.

She traveled to distant lands,

and visited wilderness no one had yet explored.

She discovered that the plains were much too windy,

the mountains
much too cold,

and the oceans
much too wet.

Finally, after much searching,
she happened upon a place she could call her own,

a pedestal of perfect size, color, and proportion.

And there she stands with pride, continuing to grow
taller and smarter each and every day.

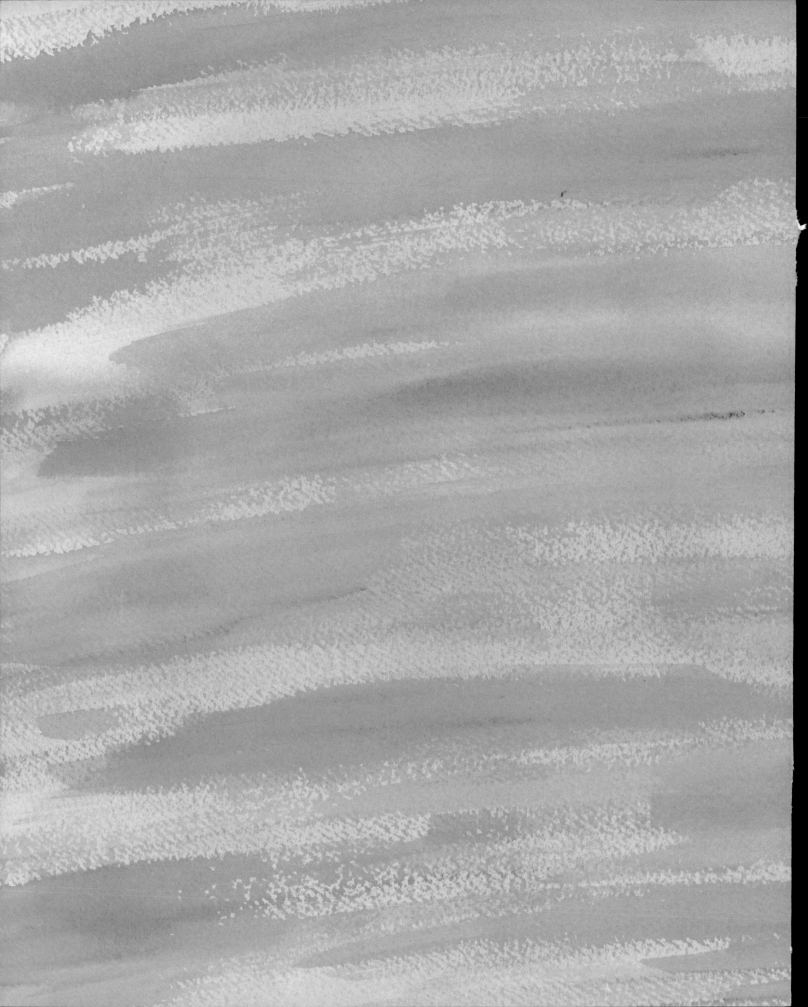